Sasha Goes to America

Adapted from The Shimmigrant

MARJY MARJ

For Keona - Big Mama's biggest fan
-MM

For Jennel
-FF

Sasha Goes to America

Written By
MARJY MARJ

Illustrated By
Fleance Forkuo

TRIPLE A PRESS BOOKS

Welcome to Book 1 of the Young Shimmigrant Series
This is a story about 12-year-old Sasha Badu's perseverance as a
housemaid in Ghana and eventual immigration to America.

Note: In Ghana, America is known as Yankey or Aburokyire
(the land beyond the corn).

Once upon a time, in a village close to Kumasi - Ghana, there was a brilliant young girl named Sasha Badu.

She lived with her Mama, Papa, and siblings.

The family enjoyed sharing stories about the big city and the village doctor's family.

The doctor's wife was called Auntie Sasha.
She drove a nice white car.

Sasha's parents dreamed that one day, their daughter will drive a nice car like Auntie Sasha.

And so they named their daughter after her.

When Sasha was 12 years old, a rich woman named Mrs. Taylor, visited the village doctor.

She was interested in recruiting a young girl to serve as a housemaid in Accra - the big city.

When Sasha's parents heard about Mrs. Taylor's request, they decided to negotiate for a job and an education for their daughter.

After Mrs. Taylor agreed to enroll Sasha in school, Mama and Papa prepared Sasha for the journey.

They thought that by sending Sasha to the big city, they were giving her an opportunity to succeed in life.

Life in the big city was harder than Sasha expected. She did chores, went to school, and came back home to do more chores.

Although she lived in a big house, she missed the village and her family.

A year after Sasha moved to Accra, Mrs. Taylor's sister, Mrs. Abban came to visit from America.

She was impressed by Sasha's hard work and offered to take her to America.

When Sasha's family heard about Mrs. Abban's offer, they were very happy.

To the family, a move to America meant that one day, Sasha was going to build a mansion in the village.

She was a step closer to owning a car and becoming successful.

Within a few weeks, Sasha and the Abbans began their journey to America.

They traveled on an airplane.

Sasha dreamed about her future on the flight.

One day, she was going to graduate from college and go on a shopping spree.

After about 11 hours on the plane, the flight landed in New York.

On arrival, Sasha was uncomfortable about lying to the airport officials.

Although she didn't understand why the Abbans changed her name for the journey, she played along by answering to Yvonne, the name in her passport.

After going through the immigration line, Sasha and the family headed to the luggage pick-up area.

She noticed that the people at the airport spoke different languages and were from different races.

When they exited the airport, they were welcomed by 2 men with name signs.

The men helped the family load the luggage into a black van.

At long last, the Abbans and Sasha were headed home.

As they drove through New York city, Sasha was surprised to see so many tall buildings.

The buildings looked like the ones that she had seen in movies.

Within 2 hours, they arrived at their destination.

When Sasha stepped out of the van, she smiled and looked up at the clear blue sky.

This was America, known as Yankey.

The land beyond the corn.

AUTHOR'S NOTE

When I was 9 years old, I played the role of a maid servant in a school play. My name was Akosua Dor. Through Akosua Dor, I learned about child labor and the sacrifices of parents who seek a better life for their children.

Although Sasha's story varies from that of Akosua Dor, it does highlight the plight of parents living in poverty, who are willing to lose their children in order to offer them a better life.

Like Sasha, I traveled to America from Ghana. However, I was lucky to come to America legally, under my own name.

Sasha, on the other hand, was brought to America with false documents. She had no idea that she was an undocumented immigrant. Neither did she realize the child labor laws that her employers disregarded.

Children do not deserve to be maltreated or misused. My hope for our world is for all children to have the opportunity to thrive.

The stories shared by immigrants tell us that individuals make sacrifices to travel to America.

May we be the ones to lend a helping hand and listen to those stories.

ACKNOWLEDGEMENTS

To Maa and Daa who sacrificed and sold their land for me to come to America.

To Mummy and Daddy for their prayers and support

To Boss Kofi and Adom who continue to be my sounding board.

To my family and uncle Kofi who welcomed me to America.

To Fleance Forkuo, for sharing his talent and skills.

To The Shimmigrant launch crew - Hajia Meimuna, Dr. Eliza, Kirsten, Loreta, Dot, Dr. Morkor, Rachel, Lillian, Evelyn and Aso - for their steadfast support.

To my sister authors Rosemond Owens, Aba Andah and Dr. Maame Norman and to my Diversity, Equity and Inclusion partner Michel Stone - for listening to and supporting my ideas.

To the numerous fans of The Shimmigrant who have welcomed me into their world.

To the distributors, bookstores, and all who speak up for HUMANITY.

I THANK YOU FROM THE BOTTOM OF MY HEART.

TOGETHER, WE CAN GO FAR.

ABOUT THE AUTHOR

Marjy Marj is a Ghanaian American writer based in South Carolina. Sasha Goes to America is her first book for young readers.

ABOUT THE ILLUSTRATOR

Born in the Brong Ahafo region, Fleance Forkuo is a Ghanaian artist based in Accra, Ghana. A graduate of Kumasi Anglican High School, he attended Christian Service University College. Fleance loves to motivate children through art. He is grateful to his parents - Felix and Angelina Forkuo for encouraging him to keep drawing. He credits Nana Opoku Amponsah, Nana Asante, and his sister - Jennel for inspiring him to produce authentic art. Fleance gives God the glory for his artistic talent.

NEXT IN THE SERIES

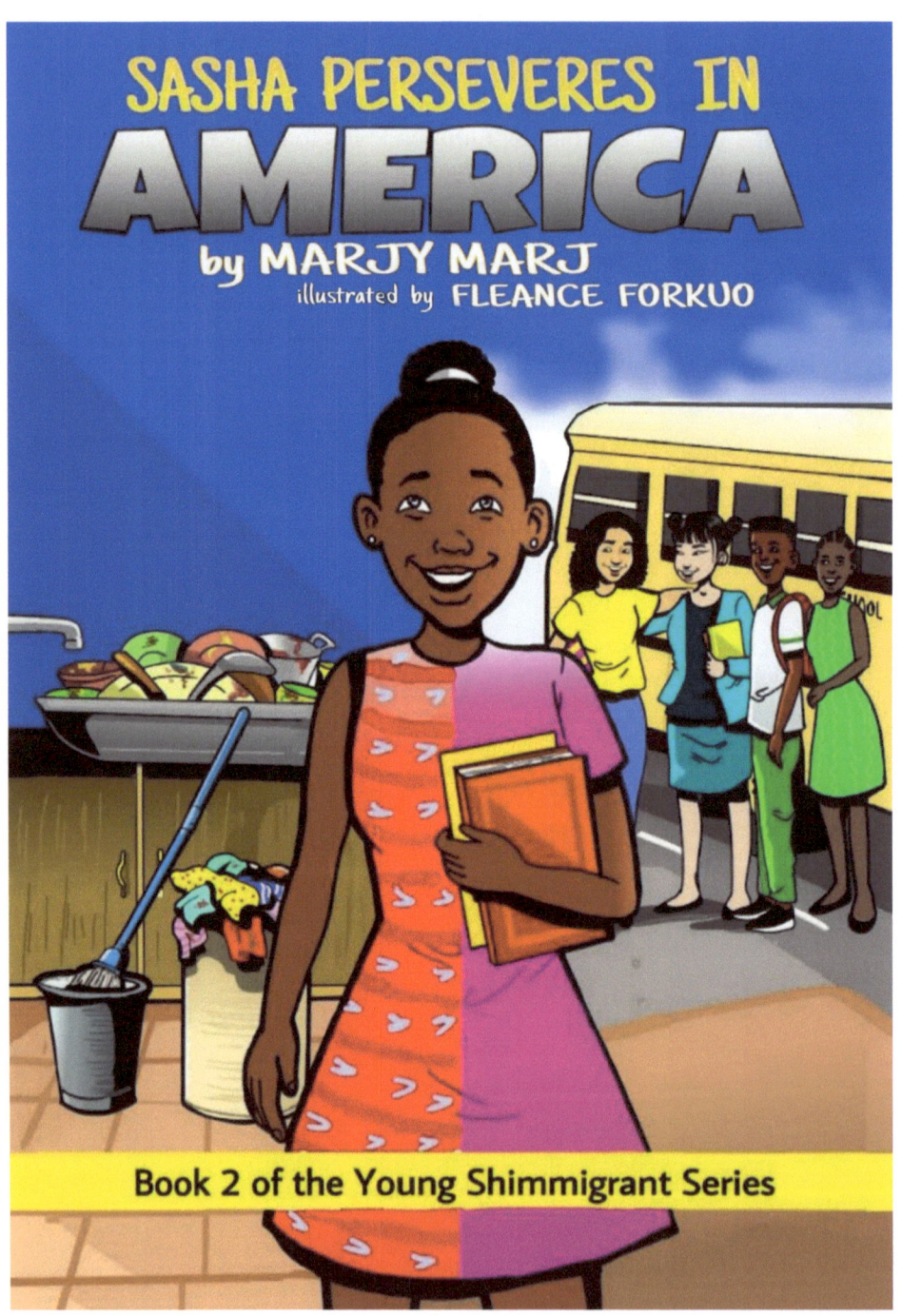

SASHA PERSEVERES IN AMERICA

by MARJY MARJ

illustrated by FLEANCE FORKUO

Book 2 of the Young Shimmigrant Series

www.ingramcontent.com/pod-product-compliance
Lightning Source LLC
Chambersburg PA
CBHW042210170626
46815CB00013B/263